Mollie Whuppie and the Giant

Retold by

Robin Muller

Scholastic Canada Ltd.

Lovingly dedicated to my nieces
Sara and Sophia,
and to my dear friends
Margie Brown and Michael Burrell.

The illustrations for this book were drawn in ink applied with a toothbrush and paintbrush, then coloured with Laurentian coloured pencils.

Canadian Cataloguing in Publication Data
Muller, Robin
    Mollie Whuppie and the giant

ISBN 0-590-74036-9

I. Title.

PS8576.U44M65 1993   jC813'.54   C92-094627-5
PZ7.M85M65 1993

6 5 4 3 2 1   Printed in Canada   3 4 5 6/9

ong, long ago in a faraway land, there lived a man and his wife who were so poor that they could not feed their children. In despair, they took their three little daughters deep into the woods and left them there.

The forest was huge and the trees bent and old. Soon the children were lost. Tess, the oldest, put her arms around her sisters and sobbed.

"Don't be afraid," said the youngest daughter, whose name was Mollie Whuppie. "When it gets dark, we will be able to follow the stars. Sooner or later we will find our way out of the forest."

Soon darkness gathered. The trees became as black as crows' wings. But above them, the stars glistened. Bravely the children set out to walk towards the North Star.

"I'm so tired," complained Tess. "I wish we could rest."

"I'm starving," said Bridie, the middle sister.

"We mustn't stop," said Mollie Whuppie firmly. "Once daylight comes, we will not know which way to go."

The children struggled on until they came to a path. It led them to an enormous old house.

"What sort of person would live here?" asked Tess fearfully.

"It looks like a prison," said Bridie, shivering.

"There's only one way to find out," said Mollie Whuppie. She marched boldly up to the door and knocked.

Slowly the door opened and a big, ugly woman peered out at them.

"What do you want?" she demanded.

"We're sorry to bother you, ma'am," said Mollie, "but we are lost in the woods. All we want is a bite to eat and a roof for the night. We won't be any trouble."

"Go away," said the woman. "My husband is a giant and he eats little children for breakfast. He'll be coming home very soon."

"Oh, please let us come in for a few minutes," begged Mollie. "My sisters are fainting from hunger and cold. Please let us in just long enough to get warm. We'll leave before the giant comes home."

Reluctantly the woman let Mollie and her sisters in and sat them before the fire. She gave them fresh-baked bread and hot milk. "Eat quickly," she said, "or you will rue the day you set foot in this place."

The giant's three cruel daughters came in to see the visitors.

"My father has a sword that can chop down a tree with one blow," said the smallest. "If he finds you here, he will chop you up in little pieces for a snack."

"My father takes gold from travellers in the forest," said the middle sister. "If you don't have gold, he will boil you for soup."

"My father has a ring of invisibility," said the oldest. "When he wishes on it, no one can see him. Maybe he's already standing right behind you, just waiting to grab you and gobble you up!"

Tess and Bridie gasped and looked around. The giant's daughters held their sides and rolled on the floor with laughter.

Amid the noise and laughter, no one heard the sound of great, heavy footsteps approaching. Suddenly the door burst open and a dreadful voice said:

Fee, fie, grunt and groan,
I am ready for blood and bone.

4

The giant glared at the girls. "Who have we here, wife?" he asked.

"Oh," said the woman, " 'tis only three little girls who were lost and hungry. I shall send them on their way immediately."

"No, no!" said the giant, twisting his face into a smile. "Let them stay. They can sleep with our own little daughters tonight."

After an enormous meal, he called the children to him. He put chains of gold around the necks of his own children, but on the necks of Mollie and her sisters he hung necklaces of straw.

"Off to bed with you now," he said with an evil grin. "Sleep tight."

When everyone was asleep, Mollie took the gold chains from the necks of the giant's daughters and the straw necklaces from her own and her sisters' necks. She gave the giant's daughters the straw necklaces, and on herself and her sisters she put the gold chains.

Later that night the door opened quietly, and in the darkness the giant felt the sleeping children. Those with necklaces of straw he threw into his leather sack and took down to the larder to be cooked for his breakfast.

When the giant was gone, Mollie woke her sisters and told them not to make a sound. As quietly as moonbeams they slipped out of the house, then ran through the forest until dawn lit the sky.

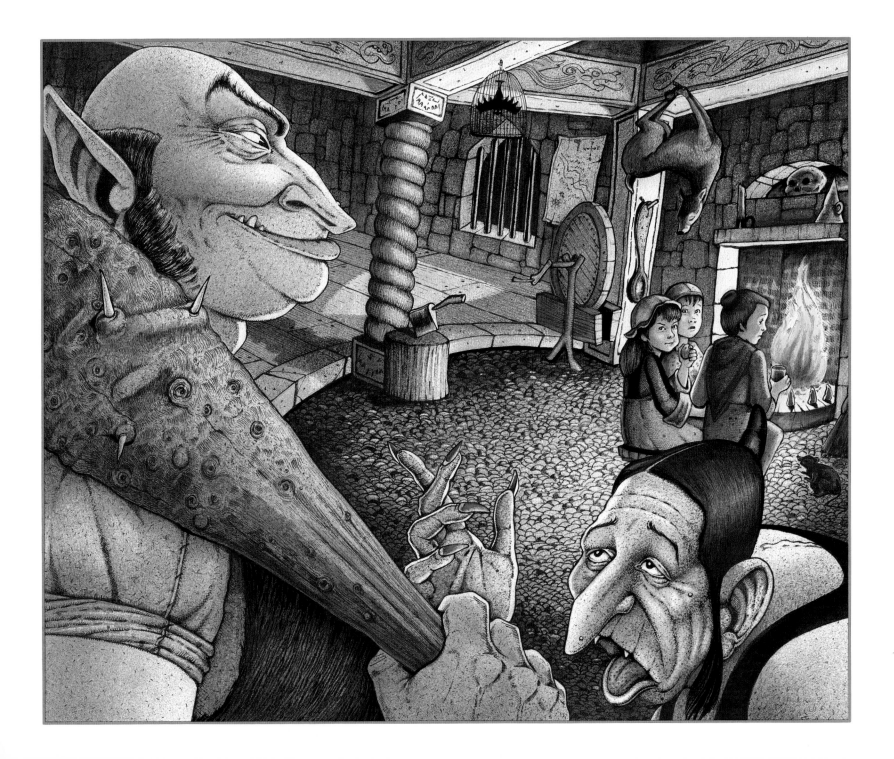

At the edge of the woods, they came to a huge gorge with a mighty river boiling over the rocks below. There was no way to cross except on a bridge made of a single strand of hair. Beyond the gorge lay green meadows, and in the distance they could see a palace shining in the morning light.

"Oh," gasped Tess, "that palace is as lovely as a dream. But how can we get to it? The bridge looks as if it wouldn't hold a fly!"

"Please think of something," said Bridie. "If we don't hurry, the giant will follow us here and eat us for his lunch."

Mollie stood at the very edge of the gorge and looked down. The sight of the water swirling and frothing around the rocks below made her dizzy. Then she looked at the Bridge of One Hair shimmering in the sunlight like spiders' silk.

"This is no ordinary hair," she said, testing it with her foot. "I think it's magic. I'm going to try to cross."

Fixing her gaze on a tower of the shining palace, Mollie let one foot slide out on the hair, then the other. Moments later she was swaying high above the gorge, with nothing to support her except her own courage.

To her amazement, the hair beneath her feet felt wide and solid. "It *is* magic!" she exclaimed, running to the other side as sure-footed as an acrobat. "Come on over," she shouted to her sisters. "It's easy. Just don't look down."

But they were too frightened to try, so Mollie ran back. "I will get you across," she said. "I will carry you piggyback. But you must keep your eyes tightly closed. I will tell you when it's safe to open them."

8

Tess screwed up her eyes so tightly they hurt, and clung to Mollie with all her might as her little sister carried her across the gorge. In a few moments Mollie returned for Bridie.

No sooner were they safely across than they heard a shout like a thunderclap. The giant stood on the other side, shaking his fist. Not daring to step on the Bridge of One Hair, he bellowed across the gorge:

Woe to you, Mollie Whuppie,
You will rue my loss and pain.
Woe to you, Mollie Whuppie,
If you dare come back again.

Mollie laughed, swinging her golden chain in the air. She called back to him:

Rant and rave, you stupid knave,
You can't scare a pack of fleas.
Rant and rave, you stupid knave,
I'll be back whene'er I please.

Then she ran after her sisters, who had fled from the sight of the giant. They followed a path that wound through meadows and farmlands towards the palace.

The three sisters walked up to the palace through beautiful gardens, where peacocks roamed the paths and birds of paradise fluttered in the trees. At the top of a huge flight of steps stood guards dressed in crimson cloth and carrying halberds of burnished silver.

Mollie Whuppie marched boldly up the steps.

"Halt!" ordered the guards. "Who are you and what do you want?"

"We mean no harm," said Mollie. "We were lost in the forest and have just escaped from a giant."

When the guards had heard their story, they ushered the children into the great hall of the palace, where the king was walking with the queen and the little prince. Sorrow lay across the king's face like a great shadow.

"Don't be afraid, children," the king said. "What brings you to my palace?"

He listened to Mollie's story with great attention, and as she spoke, his eyes began to shine with joy.

"Mollie Whuppie," he said, "you have succeeded where my bravest knights have failed. For years the giant of the forest has been robbing travellers of their gold and stealing little children to be cooked for his breakfast. And although many valiant men have ridden out to destroy him, no one has ever returned alive. No one except you and your sisters!"

He placed his hand on Mollie's shoulder. "My dear, you are clever indeed. You are probably the only one who can outwit the giant. If you will go back and steal his magic sword, which has killed so many of my men, I promise you that your sister Tess shall marry the knight of her choice."

Mollie looked at the king with sparkling eyes. "That would make Tess very happy," she said. "I will certainly do my best."

Back Mollie went across the Bridge of One Hair, through the forest to the giant's house. When no one was watching, she crept silently in through the huge door and tiptoed up the stone stairs to the giant's bedroom. She slid under his bed and waited.

In her hiding place, she began to feel a little sorry that she had come. Above her, the giant's reed mattress bulged like a vast lumpy roof held by a network of ropes. Around her, fluffy balls of dust and pieces of reed covered the floor. The sour, mouldy smell almost made her sick. She bit her lip and lay as still as she could.

Very soon the giant came home. Mollie could hear his heavy footsteps as he entered the house, and his monstrous chewing and belching as he wolfed down his supper. At last he climbed the stairs to go to bed. With a weary sigh, he took off his belt and hung his sword on the bedpost.

Mollie hardly dared breathe until she heard the giant snoring above her. Then she crept out and with all her strength pulled the magic sword from its sheath. It was very heavy, but she held it firmly and quietly tiptoed from the room.

No sooner had she set foot on the stairs than she heard an angry shout. Mollie flew like the wind, with the giant's footsteps pounding behind her. At any moment she expected to feel his huge hand on her shoulder.

She even thought she would have to throw the sword away in order to save herself, but as she ran, she suddenly realized that it was growing lighter and lighter. Soon it was no heavier than a feather.

With the giant's breath almost tickling her neck, Mollie raced to the Bridge of One Hair. As she sped across the shimmering thread, the giant skidded to a halt at the very edge of the gorge. He stamped his foot and howled with rage:

Woe to you, Mollie Whuppie,
You will rue my loss and pain.
Woe to you, Mollie Whuppie,
If you dare come back again.

Safe and sound on the other side, Mollie laughed with happiness. She waved the sword and shouted back to the giant:

Grump, grump, you gormless lump,
Stupid threats don't frighten me.
Grump, grump, you gormless lump,
I'll be back, just wait and see!

Then she took the magic sword to the palace. The king was overjoyed. "Thanks to you, Mollie Whuppie," he said, "the giant has lost his most terrible weapon." True to his word, he allowed Tess to select a handsome knight, who promised to love her all his life.

But the king's joy did not last long, and soon he was looking as sad as ever. "I cannot help thinking of all the people the giant has robbed," he sighed. "They are now poor and hungry. If you would go back and get me the giant's purse of gold, I could return the money they lost. You are clever enough to do it, Mollie, even though he keeps the purse under his pillow. If you will get it, I promise you that your sister Bridie shall marry the knight of her choice."

"Well," said Mollie thoughtfully, "I will certainly try."

Once again Mollie returned to the giant's house and hid under his bed. Once again she almost choked breathing the dust and the mouldy smell. "I wish the giant would clean his room," she thought.

Before long, the door opened and the giant came thumping in. He sat down on the edge of the bed and pulled off his huge boots. "I wish he would change his socks too," Mollie thought, wrinkling her nose.

The giant pulled the magic purse of gold out of his jerkin and stuffed it under the pillow. Soon he was snoring thunderously. His hand was directly above the purse, and Mollie knew that she could never pull it out unless he rolled over. But he slept for hours without twitching a muscle.

Finally Mollie found a long piece of reed under the bed and very softly touched his cheek. The giant grunted and slapped at the reed. Then she tickled his nose. He gave an enormous sneeze and rolled over with a great sigh, burying his face in the covers.

Mollie reached up. Gently she pulled the purse free.

Once more Mollie heard the giant awaken, and once more she had to race for her life. With only seconds to spare, she dashed across the Bridge of One Hair and stopped to catch her breath on the other side.

The giant's face was purple with rage. He stamped his foot so hard that the earth trembled. At the top of his mighty voice he roared:

Woe to you, Mollie Whuppie,
You will rue my loss and pain.
Woe to you, Mollie Whuppie,
If you dare come back again.

Safe on the other side, Mollie laughed and did a little dance. She swung the bag of gold to and fro and called back:

Scream and shout, you ugly lout,
Say goodbye to what you lose.
Scream and shout, you ugly lout,
I'll come back whene'er I choose.

The king was delighted with Mollie's success. True to his word, he let Bridie choose a knight to be her husband. She picked a fine and jovial young man, who was overjoyed that she liked him.

But soon the king's sadness returned. When Mollie asked what was troubling him, he said, "Thanks to you, Mollie, the giant has lost his sword and his gold. But while he has the ring of invisibility, he can still do terrible things to travellers in the forest. If you will go back and get it for me, you too may choose a husband — anyone you wish, be he the son of the noblest lord in my kingdom."

Mollie smiled and replied, "Who is the noblest lord in the kingdom, your majesty?"

The king looked thoughtful. "Well, that is hard to say. There are many noble lords."

"I know who it is," said Mollie. "It is you. And the son of the noblest lord is the crown prince."

The king looked surprised, then laughed. "You are right. And if you bring me the ring, I promise that you shall marry my son."

As she lay under the giant's bed for the third time, Mollie was surprised to find that the floor was clean. "I hope no one noticed that I hid here," she thought. But before she could move, the giant came in and flopped down on the bed.

Soon he lay in a deep sleep, but the night was almost gone before his arm moved free of the covers and hung down beside her head. She could see the ring gleaming in the darkness, as big as a bracelet.

Mollie's fingers softly reached around the ring and gently turned it. Each twist tugged it a little lower on the giant's finger. Finally it slid across his knuckle and lay in her hand. She slipped it into the pocket of her apron.

Wriggling out from under the bed, Mollie noticed that the snoring had stopped. She rolled over to look up, and gasped. Staring down at her was the giant, a horrible grin on his face. He grabbed her with a grip that would have squashed an oak tree.

"So I have you at last!" he gloated. "My wife told me that you had been hiding under my bed. Now I've tricked you before you could trick me." His laugh sounded like rocks tumbling down a mountainside.

"Mollie Whuppie," said the giant, "tell me this: had I treated you the way you have treated me, what would you do to me?"

"I would throw you in a big sack," replied Mollie quickly, "and put a dog and a cat in with you. Then I would hang the sack on the wall while I went to the woods to find the biggest and thickest stick I could. Then I would beat the sack until you were dead."

The giant's face lit up with a wicked smile. "Very well," he said, "that is exactly what I shall do to you."

He got a sack and put Mollie into it, then threw in a dog and a cat. With a cheerful whistle, he hung it up on the wall while he went off to the forest to find a stick. As soon as he was gone, Mollie very sweetly began to sing:

If only you could see
The things that I can see,
How happy you would be,
How happy you would be.

In the kitchen, the giant's wife could hear her singing. She came out to where the sack was hanging. "Mollie Whuppie," she said, "please tell me what it is that you can see in there."

But Mollie ignored her and continued to sing, as carefree as a lark. Finally the giant's wife got so curious that she begged to know what Mollie could see.

"Oh, all right," said Mollie, "But I can't tell you. You will just have to see for yourself. Go and get a pair of scissors and a needle and thread. Cut a hole in the sack and I will let you in."

When the woman had done as she was told, Mollie jumped down out of the sack. She helped the giant's wife get into it and sewed up the hole. Of course the woman could see nothing inside the sack and soon shouted to be let out. Without a word, Mollie hid behind the door.

Soon the giant returned with a tree trunk in his hand. He took down the sack and began to beat it soundly.

"It's me, you fool!" shouted his wife. But what with the barking of the dog and the screeching of the cat, he could not hear her.

"You great pea-brained oaf," she howled. "You monstrous idiot!" But still the giant kept beating her.

Since Mollie did not want the old woman to die, she stepped out from behind the door and raced past the giant towards the forest. Astounded, he threw down his tree trunk and started after her.

Mollie fled like a startled deer. Fearing the ring of invisibility might bounce out of her pocket, she slipped it onto her wrist.

"Oh, I wish I were invisible," she gasped as she ran. Then she tripped on a tree root and went sprawling to the ground. "Oh, no!"

But the giant ran right past her as though she did not exist. "He can't see me!" Mollie exclaimed. "The ring worked!"

She climbed to her feet and walked back to the giant's house. When she got there, she took off the ring and said to the giant's wife, "I will let you out of the sack if you promise me one thing."

"Anything!" said the woman, who was black and blue all over.

"If ever the giant does not return, will you vow to make this house a shelter for travellers? Will you feed them and give them a clean place to sleep and send them safely on their way?"

"Gladly, gladly," promised the giant's wife.

"And remember," warned Mollie sternly, "cook breakfast for children, not children for breakfast."

"I will!" said the woman. Molly snipped the thread and let her out.

At the Bridge of One Hair the giant was waiting. Mollie put on the ring of invisibility and made her wish. Boldly she marched up to the giant, who could not see even the shadow of her footsteps.

When she was directly behind him, she slipped off the ring. "Boo!" she said in her loudest voice. The giant jumped and spun around. Mollie dodged between his legs and ran across the bridge.

"Oh, giant," she called from the other side, "did you lose anything?" She held up the ring.

The giant was furious. "That is the very last thing you will steal from me, Mollie Whuppie," he screamed, shaking his fists.

"You are right," said Mollie, laughing.

The earth trembled as the giant stamped his feet in rage. Suddenly the ground gave way. With a terrible scream, he went hurtling down to the river below and hit the water with a tremendous splash. When the spray cleared, all that could be seen was a great giant-shaped rock in the midst of the raging torrent.

Mollie ran back to the palace.

"You've done it again!" said the king, his eyes bright with joy. "You've brought me the ring of invisibility!"

"And the giant is dead," said Mollie. "He will never hurt travellers again."

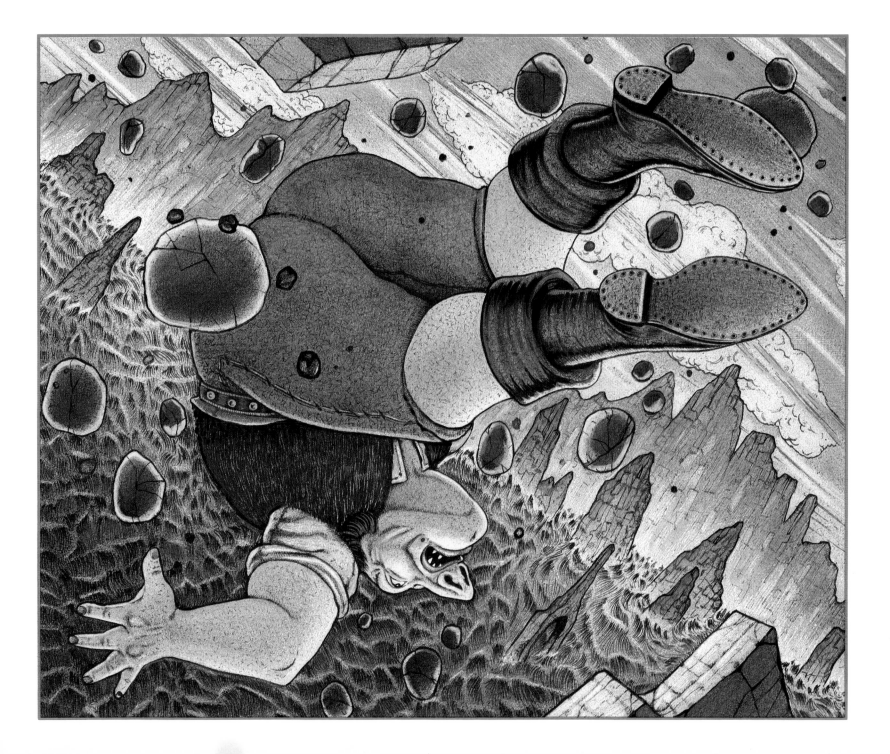

The king's son was overjoyed at the thought of having such a clever girl for his wife. But on the day of the wedding Mollie was nowhere to be found. A note to the king was pinned to her pillow.

Your Majesty:

I thought I would like to see the world before I wed, so I have borrowed a horse and bridle to carry me on my way. Please give my love to my sisters and ask the prince to wait. I will return one day.

Your servant,
Mollie Whuppie

The prince did wait, and on a sunny morning some time later Mollie returned and wed him. They spent the rest of their lives in great happiness, and the prince never tired of listening to Mollie tell of all her wonderful adventures.